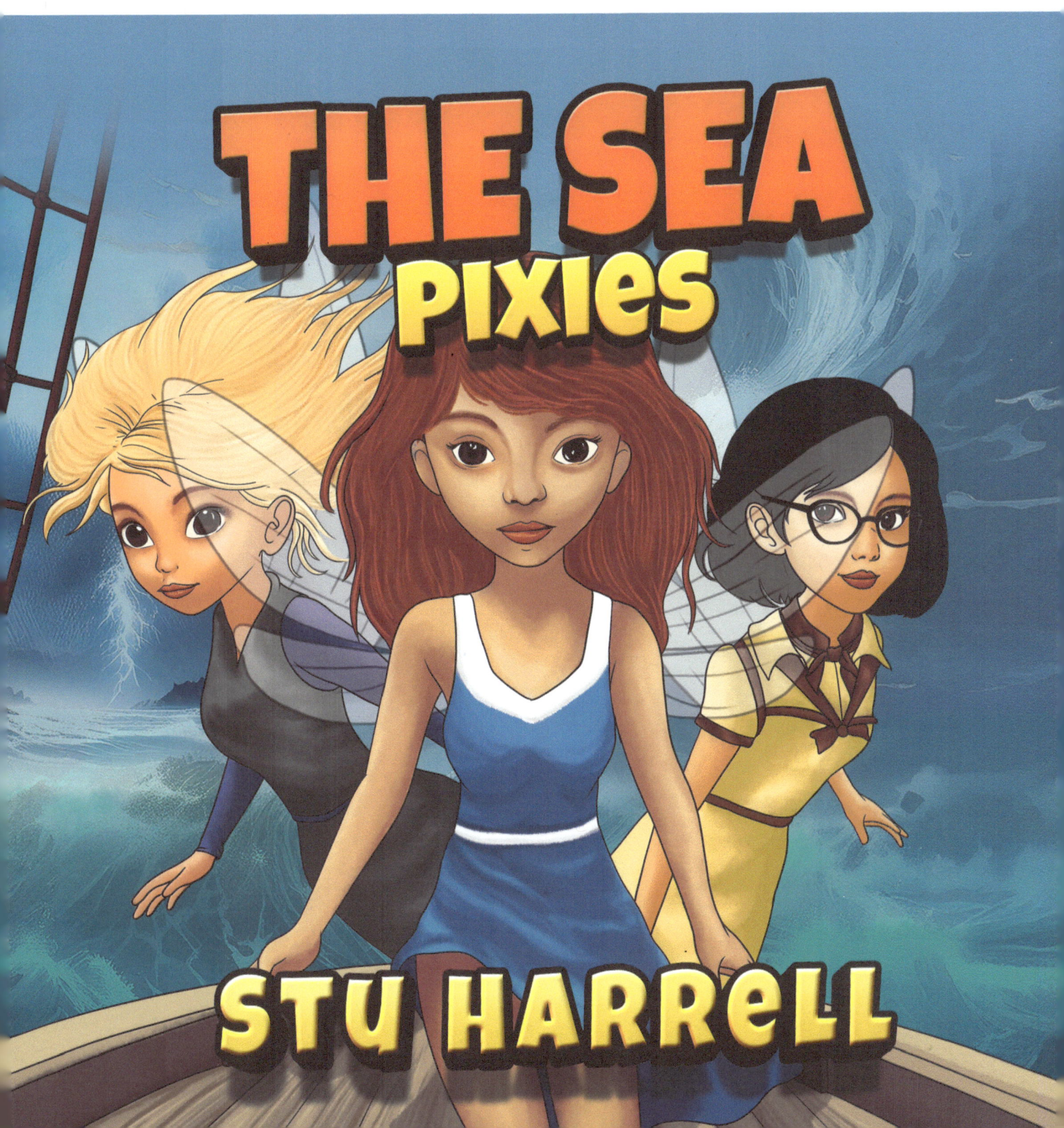

Copyright © 2024 by Stu Harrell.

All rights reserved. No part of this publication may be reproduced, distributed, or transmitted in any form or by any electronic or mechanical means, including information storage and retrieval systems, without a prior written permission from the publisher, except by reviewers, who may quote brief passages in a review, and certain other noncommercial uses permitted by the copyright law.

ISBN: 979-8-89228-281-9   (Paperback)
ISBN: 979-8-89228-285-7   (Hardcover)
ISBN: 979-8-89228-280-2   (eBook)

Printed in the United States of America

We're bound around Cape Horn today,
Raise a glass before we set sail,
To the Pixies who'll guide our way

She swoops to aid the mizzenmast,
But a hint of rum makes her grin—
Captain Morgan's legacy from the past.

She knows every creature 'neath the tide,
A master of stars and sextants too—
Fast as the winds she'll always guide.

With a strange celestial gleam,
Called forth these Pixie spirits,
To guide us through the darkest dream.

Through rain-soaked, sparkling eyes,
While ever-stressed starboard braced,
Held firm by Stormy's fearless ties.

Through swirling seas and stormy night,
The ship rocked but held its course,
Guided by Gale's steady light.

With Pixies' help, our course set free,
Now press ahead to Old Cathay,
To grasp a load of China tea.

Milton Keynes UK
Ingram Content Group UK Ltd.
UKHW051335170924
1695UKWH00001BD/1